Chapters

Ghostly Football

'Hey, Granda . . .' Seamus threw down his book. 'How's about coming out with me on one of my night-time walks?'

'Ah no,' said his scaredy granda. 'It's cosy here by the fire.'

But Seamus grabbed his torch and his bag, and his granda had to follow him.

> There it is!

'What's that sound?' whispered Granda.
But there was nothing to be heard but the
hooting of an owl.

Then, 'What's that light?' moaned Granda.
But there was nothing to be seen but the
twinkling of a thousand stars.

Then, 'Help!' yelped Granda. They'd come to an old barn and what did they hear from inside but the spookiest sound, like a cross between a mighty yawn and a '*Wooooooooooo!*'

'Let's go home and have a nice pot of tea,' whispered Granda.

Cool!

But in went Seamus, so in went his granda behind him. And what did they see but a load of fed-up ghosts.

'What's the matter?' asked Seamus.

'We're bored out of our skulls,' said a ghost. 'All we ever do for years on end is sit about going "*Woooooo!*"'

I'm bored!

'But why are you here? Why can't you rest in peace?' Granda asked.

I'm terrified!

'To tell you the truth, we're cowards,' whispered another ghost. 'We're too scared to go up to the gates of heaven in case they send us down below, into the flames of hell. So we're stuck here in this barn.'

9

Spooky soccer!

'I know what'd stop you being bored,' Seamus told him. 'And it might even give you a bit of courage, too.'

'What's that?' asked the ghost.

'Form a football team and play other ghosts!' replied Seamus with a grin.

'Sounds scary,' said Greg the Ghoul, frowning. 'We haven't played for years.'

'We'll help you get into shape,' offered

Scary!

Seamus. 'Won't we, Granda?'

So they got the ghosts doing press-ups, step-ups and running on the spot every night for a week.

'I hope you're fit enough,' said Seamus the following Friday. 'Tomorrow night you're playing in the quarter-finals of the After-life Cup!'

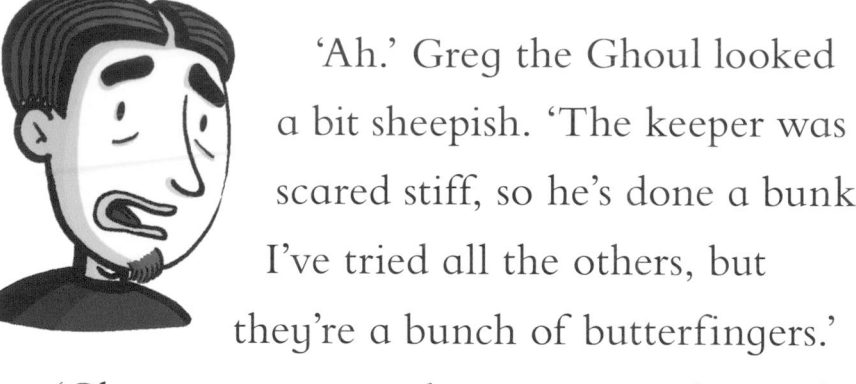

'Ah.' Greg the Ghoul looked a bit sheepish. 'The keeper was scared stiff, so he's done a bunk. I've tried all the others, but they're a bunch of butterfingers.'

'Ghosts are supposed to scare people, not be scared!' said Seamus, frowning. 'I'll be your keeper till we train someone up.'

Greg looked him up and down. 'Bit small for a goalie, aren't you?'

'I'm fast, though,' said Seamus. 'Try me!'

So first Phantom Pete had a go. Then Haunted Henry, followed by all the others.

Pow!

And finally Greg
himself took a kick.
Biff! Bash! Boot!
They whacked it
and tickled it, thumped
it and tapped it.

Seamus dived to the
left and the right, up high
and down low. And he
saved every shot.

'You're in the Spooks team, Seamus!' said
Greg, the captain. 'So who
are we up against?'

'Mouldy Milan,' replied
Seamus. 'But we'd better
do some more training.
They're dead good . . .'

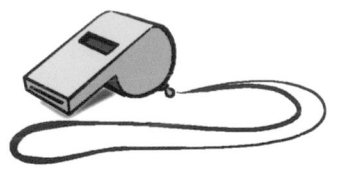

Mouldy Milan

'WHEEEE!' Granda blew the whistle and the match was on.

'Mamma mia!' laughed Luca Bonito, Milan's captain, looking at Seamus. 'Their goalie's a piccolo pixie!'

'Ha!' Tomaso Torino, their centre-forward, grinned. 'This will be easy-peasy pizza!'

Torino ran towards goal but Seamus darted out, double-quick, and stole the ball from his legs.

Seamus lobbed it high in the air to Phantom Pete, who headed it on to Haunted Henry . . .

who smashed it straight through Milan's keeper. One-nil to the Spooks!

From the re-start Bonito passed to Torino, who nudged it back to his captain, who dribbled round Phantom Pete and slipped it over to Torino again . . . who was just about to shoot, hard and fast, when Greg the Ghoul plucked up all his courage and shoulder-charged him.

'Aaiii!' Torino fell in a heap.

'WHEEEE!' Granda blew his whistle. 'Penalty kick!'

Bonito placed the ball on the spot. He walked back six paces then ran forward and hit it, hard and low.

Zap!

But Seamus had seen the captain glance to the left. He sprang to the ball just as it came flashing towards him. And somehow he managed to get his fingers to it, tipping it up and round the post.

I don't believe it!

'Aaiii!' Bonito put his head in his hands. 'Piccolo pixie's saved it!'

Seamus caught the ball from Milan's corner kick and flung it out to Greg the Ghoul, who shimmied round Torino then floated it over to Phantom Pete . . . who nudged it to Haunted Henry, and BANG! Two–nil. Half–time.

By the second half, both sets of ghosts were fading fast.

'Keep your spirits up, Spooks!' yelled Seamus. 'Don't give up the ghost!'

There were no more goals until the very last minute of the game. 'Everyone's half dead,' thought Seamus. 'I'll give it a go myself.'

He darted down the field, dribbling the ball round ghost after worn-out ghost, before launching it across to Haunted Henry and racing on towards goal.

Henry managed a beautiful overhead pass straight to Seamus, who nutted it – thump – into the top right-hand corner.

'WHEEEE!' Three-nil. Game over.

'Brave stuff, lads!' cried Greg. 'We're through to the semi-finals!'

We did it!

Spooky Semis

Phantom Pete offered to have a try at being keeper, so Seamus and his granda gave him loads of special goalie training:

running,

 diving,

making scary faces . . .

22

Then everyone fired shots at him. First
Granda had a go, then all the others.
Bash, bang, blast! They kicked it and jiggled
it, whumped it and wellied it.

Got one
at last!

And Phantom Pete charged around the
goalmouth to the left and the right, up high
and down low . . . until at last he started
saving some.

Every night that week Seamus got the Spooks doing warm-ups (and it takes a lot of warming up to warm up a ghost).

Then they practised sprinting, passing, heading the ball and throw-ins.

And the next Saturday night they were up against the Salvador Shadows from Brazil.

Seamus took Phantom Pete's place in the forward line – the Spooks weren't quite brave enough to play on their own just yet – and it was two-two in the dying seconds of the match.

Pete was doing all right in goal and the game was going to extra time. But then Greg booted the ball to Seamus . . . who did a head-over-heels bicycle kick and smashed it, slap bang, straight past the Salvador Shadows goalie.

Hooray!

'We won!' yelled the captain.

'You're in the final!' cried Seamus, delighted. 'But you're on your own from now on, lads. It's time to prove how brave you really are.'

Best Team in the Universe, Ever!

So Seamus took on the role of full-time trainer-manager. He got them doing corner kicks, the offside trap and pretending to be dead when someone kicks you (they were good at that one, being ghosts).

Go for it!

'Be brave, boys,' he yelled on match day, pacing up and down the line. 'No knees a-knocking! Don't get cold feet!'

Granda took on the role of number-one fan, roaring them on (oh, and he was the referee too, of course).

And the Spooks played out of their skins against the legendary 1892 Spurs team.

It was three-three after extra time, so it went to penalties. And Phantom Pete proved himself a lion-hearted, shot-stopping keeper by saving every single one.

Amazing! The scaredy-ba
Spooks were the
After-life champs!

'Right, lads!' cried
Seamus as Greg held up
the cup. 'You can cast off
your ghostly ghoulishness
and head on up to heaven at last.'

We're the best!

Some of the team still looked just a tiny bit
worried at the prospect of the pearly gates.

'It's all right, men,' said Greg. 'With Seamus
and his granda's
help, we've proved
we're not cowards
any more. We
can hold our
heads high and
know we're good
enough to get in.'

So they pinned their winners' medals to their see-through chests to prove what heroes they were. Then they hoisted Seamus and his granda on to their shoulders and marched to the gates of heaven, singing away.

Oh, when the Spooks go marching in,
Oh, when the Spooks go marching in,
I want to be in that number,
When the Spooks go marching in!

'Put Seamus and me down, lads!' cried Granda. 'We're not quite ready to go to heaven just yet.'

But Greg didn't hear him, with all the noise. He led his men to the gate, shouting, 'Spooks, trainer and ref!' and the saint on duty just smiled and waved them through.

Saints and Spirits

And what did they find in Heaven but a
whole load of dead footballers, playing each
other for the Saints and Spirits Cup!

So Seamus encouraged the Spooks to put up a team and they got through to the final, where they were up against the Accrington Stanley Angels.

And they beat
them, seventeen-four!

'Granda! Granda!' Seamus knew he'd better get home soon or his mum'd be frantic. But he couldn't find the old fellow anywhere.

He searched high and low and eventually heard the twang of a guitar and a couple of people crooning, one tunefully and the other not-so-tunefully. The not-so-tuneful one was Granda. He'd come across his lifelong hero, Elvis Presley, sitting on a cloud, strumming away.

Where are you?

'You ain't nothing but a hound dog,' sang Elvis. 'Crying all the time . . .'

'Howl-lll!' went Granda in less-than-perfect harmony.

You ain't never caught a rabbit, and you ain't no friend of mine!

'Did Elvis really get to heaven, Granda?' whispered Seamus. 'I thought he was a bit of a bad lad in his day.'

Elvis had overheard him. 'I sure as hickory did! Tell you what, guys – seeing as you and those buddies of yours are all so brave, why not head on down to hell and teach the Dirtbag Devils how to play soccer. I hear they're the filthiest team that ever died!'

Worst Team in the Universe, Ever!

So Seamus led the brave Spooks down to
hell and it didn't take them long to find
the Dirtbag Devils. They were cursing
and swearing, fouling and fighting.

Oi!

'Do we really have to play them, boss?' asked Greg, nervously.

'I think you'd better,' replied Seamus. 'Just to teach them some manners.'

'Well, you won't catch me being ref,' said his granda, quaking in his boots. 'That bunch would eat you alive.'

'Give me the whistle, then,' said Seamus.
And he blew it loud and long. 'WHEEEE!'
'Right, you lot!' he yelled. 'I want a good
clean game and no swearing!'

'...or you're off!'

And do you think the Devils did as they were told? They did not. They cheated and cursed, they fouled and they fought, they swore at the ref . . .

. . . who pulled out his red card and gave them their marching orders, every one of them.

By the end of the game there wasn't a single Dirtbag Devil on the pitch, and the Spooks were taking it in turns to fire into an empty net.

Hooray!

Not surprisingly, they won the match – a hundred and seventy two-nil! And Seamus nearly wore out his whistle with all the blowing he had to do.

'We beat them!'
cried Greg, hugging
Seamus and his
granda. 'Thanks to
you two we've gone
to the scariest place
there is – hell itself! – and
thrashed the craziest team there ever was.
We're brave, lads! Really brave!'

'We sure are, Captain,'
cried the rest of the
Spooks, cheering.

Greg beamed with pride. 'And now we're back off up to heaven to rest in peace for ever and ever, eh men?'

'Aye aye, Captain!'

See you, Seamus!

But when Seamus looked around, there was no sign of his granda. 'Granda! Granda!' he called. 'You can't stay down here!'

He found him sharing a cuppa with Old Nick, the number-one nasty himself. 'This tea's boiling hot!' Haven't you heard of milk here in hell?' said Seamus.

'No cows,' said Old Nick grumpily. 'They're just not evil enough.'

'Let's go, Granda,' whispered Seamus. 'This is no place for the likes of us.'

47

'Hey, Granda . . .' said Seamus. They were back home at last. 'The Spooks were good, weren't they?'

'Best team in the world,' said his granda.

'Heaven, too,' said Seamus with a laugh.

'And Hell,' added Granda as they settled down to sleep. 'Hey, leave the light on, Seamus!'

'Why's that?'

'Because even if the Spooks have found their courage, there's still one scaredy-ba left.'

'Who's that then, Granda?'

'Me!'

Good night, Seamus!

Nighty night, Granda!